For my very best friend, Ann
– S. S.

Pour Billie Marilou, qui n'a pas peur des loups
– J. D.

tiger tales
5 River Road, Suite 128, Wilton, CT 06897
Published in the United States 2019
Originally published in Great Britain 2019
by Little Tiger Press Ltd.
Text copyright © 2019 Steve Smallman
Illustrations copyright © 2019 Joëlle Dreidemy
ISBN-13: 978-1-68010-159-1
ISBN-10: 1-68010-159-5
Printed in China
LTP/1400/2661/0219
10 9 8 7 6 5 4 3 2 1

For more insight and activities, visit us at www.tigertalesbooks.com

THE WOLVES WHO CAME FOR DINNER

by STEVE SMALLMAN Illustrated by JOËLLE DREIDEMY

Wolf and Little Lamb were
the very best of friends.

But the other animals who lived
in the forest were worried.

They just couldn't understand how
a wolf and a lamb could get along.

Is that a lamb
and a wolf?

Together?

He'll gobble
her up!

"Let's invite the bunnies for a playdate!" suggested Wolf.
"Yippee!" cheered Little Lamb.
So they spent all morning baking carrot cupcakes.

But when Wolf opened the door and said, "Snack time!" . . . all the rabbits ran away!

It's a big, bad wolf!

Quick! Hop it!

Aaaaaaaaaagh!

Wolf sat down on the doorstep.
"I'm not a bad wolf," he sighed. "I'm a GOOD wolf!"

"Yes, you are!" agreed Little Lamb. "Can we still play now?"
"Yes!" cried Wolf. "And if the bunnies won't
come to us, we'll go to them!"

"Maybe they'll let us join their game!"
Wolf whispered.
     But when they tried to play
hide-and-seek . . .

It's that
wolf again!

Ready or
not, HERE I COME!

. . . Wolf couldn't understand why the only animal he found was Little Lamb.

"Your friends are too good at hiding," sighed Wolf. "Looks like it's just you and me."

"Me and you!" beamed Little Lamb, giving Wolf a big hug.

"I know!" cried Wolf. "We'll invite *my* friends over to meet *you*, Little Lamb!"

But when Gripper, Nipper, and Growler arrived, they were starving.

"We love a little lamb!" they cried, licking their lips.

"Yes, well, I love Little Lamb, too!" said Wolf crossly. "And that's why you can't eat her! Now, how about some vegetable soup?"

After dinner,
Wolf read them
a story.

Little Lamb held
Gripper's hand
when it got to
the scary part.

And by the end,
they were all snuggled
up together, fast asleep.

A few days later, Wolf and Little Lamb were playing by the river. "Don't worry," said Wolf. "I've got you!"

That wolf has that lamb!

"Oh, no!" the forest creatures cried.
"We have to help her!"

"LEAVE HER ALONE!" the animals yelled.
Wolf was so surprised that he fell into the river
with a SPLASH!

Little Lamb helped Wolf out of the water.

"It's not time to swim, Wolf," she said. "It's snack time!"

Wolf sighed and took Little Lamb's paw in his as he sadly plodded home.

But when they arrived, Gripper, Nipper, and Growler were waiting by the door.

Oh, no!

GASP!

More wolves!

Yippeee!

"I told you!" Wolf snapped. "You can't eat Little Lamb!"
"We know!" called Gripper. "But could we have
another story?"
"And a *sleepover*?" added Nipper and Growler.
Wolf smiled and let them in.

And after more **delicious** vegetable soup,

silly stories,

and bedtime snuggles...

everyone fell *fast asleep*.

"We'll rush in on the count of three!" declared Fox. "One . . . two . . ."

The forest creatures burst in, but

AAA-OOOOOO!

an eerie howl

stopped them in their tracks!

It was Little Lamb!
She gave the animals a hard stare
and said, "Don't hurt my Wolf!"

"Would it help if we ate some of them?" suggested Growler.
"Don't hurt my friends!" answered Little Lamb crossly.
Everyone looked a little sheepish until Wolf said,
"How wonderful to have so many visitors!
Sleepover, anyone?"

So everyone settled down in the
warm glow of the fire, and
Wolf read them a story.

It was a story about making friends that was
funny, and exciting, and (a little bit) scary.
And at the end, like in most good stories,
they all lived happily ever after.